All Aboard to Work—Choo-Choo!

By Carol Roth   Illustrated by Steve Lavis

Albert Whitman & Company, Chicago, Illinois

Library of Congress Cataloging-in-Publication Data

Roth, Carol.
All aboard to work—choo-choo! / by Carol Roth ; illustrated by Steve Lavis.
p. cm.
Summary: Animal mothers and fathers with various professions take the train to work and
return at the end of the day to spend time with their children.
ISBN 978-0-8075-0271-6
[1. Stories in rhyme. 2. Railroad trains—Fiction. 3. Work—Fiction. 4. Animals—Fiction.]
I. Lavis, Steve, ill. II. Title.
PZ8.3.R7456Al 2009   [E]—dc22   2008055707

The design is by Carol Gildar.

For more information about Albert Whitman & Company,
please visit our web site at www.albertwhitman.com.

To my precious grandsons, Jake, Ethan, and Adam, with love.—C.R.

For Sarah, who likes to work with words.—S.L.

"Kiss, kiss," say the mommies. "I love you!"

"Hug, hug," say the daddies. "Love you, too!"

"Off to work we go . . . Bye-bye!"

"Off to the train . . . Bye-bye!"

Here comes the choo-choo down the track.
Clickety, clickety, clickety-clack.

"ALL ABOARD!" to work . . . choo-choo!
Chug-a-chug-a-choo-choo-choo!

The first one on
is Fearless Cat.
See his bright
red fireman's hat!

"ALL ABOARD!" to work . . . choo-choo!
Chug-a-chug-a-choo-choo-choo!

The second one on
is Nifty Newt,
dressed up in his
business suit.
A newt in his suit,
a cat with his hat.

"ALL ABOARD!" to work . . . choo-choo!
Chug-a-chug-a-choo-choo-choo!

The third one on
   is Dolly Duck.
She'd like to fix your
   car or truck.
A duck who
   loves trucks,
a newt in his suit,
a cat with his hat.

"ALL ABOARD!" to work . . . choo-choo!
Chug-a-chug-a-choo-choo-choo!

The fourth one on is Caring Bear,
healing sick ones everywhere.
A bear who cares,
a duck who loves trucks,
a newt in his suit,
a cat with his hat.

DR BEAR

"ALL ABOARD!" to work . . . choo-choo!
Chug-a-chug-a-choo-choo-choo!

The fifth one on is Officer Roo,
so proud in her suit of blue.
A roo in blue,
a bear who cares,
a duck who loves trucks,
a newt in his suit,
a cat with his hat.

CHOO-CHOO

"ALL ABOARD!" to work . . . choo-choo!
Chug-a-chug-a-choo-choo-choo!

The sixth one on is Professor Hen,
carrying her books and pen.
A hen with a pen,
a roo in blue,
a bear who cares,
a duck who loves trucks,
a newt in his suit,
a cat with his hat.

NEWT

"ALL ABOARD!" to work . . . choo-choo!
Chug-a-chug-a-choo-choo-choo!

The last one on is Gourmet Seal.
He's off to cook some yummy meals.
A seal with meals,
a hen with a pen,
a roo in blue,
a bear who cares,
a duck who loves trucks,
a newt in his suit,
a cat with his hat.

"ALL ABOARD!" to work . . . choo-choo!
Chug-a-chug-a-choo-choo-choo!

All day long they work so hard
while the train waits in the station yard.

And when the workday finally ends,
the train will bring them home again.

Here comes the
choo-choo down
the track.
Moms and dads
are coming back!
A seal with meals,
a hen with a pen,
a roo in blue,
a bear who cares,
a duck who
loves trucks,
a newt in
his suit,
a cat with
his hat.

Riding the train back home . . . choo-choo!
Chug-a-chug-a-choo-choo-choo!

"Kiss, kiss," say the mommies. "I missed you!"
"Hug, hug," say the daddies. "Missed you, too!"

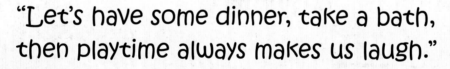

"Let's have some dinner, take a bath,
then playtime always makes us laugh."

"We'll read a bedtime story, too.
We'll cuddle up, say 'I love you.'
We'll tuck you in all snug and tight.
Then kiss again and say good night."